Zero the Hero

To: Edgar Miller Students

Venetia Poplar Brown
2/8/02

Zero the Hero

Venetia Poplar Brown

VANTAGE PRESS
New York

FIRST EDITION

Published by Vantage Press, Inc.
516 West 34th Street, New York, New York 10001

Manufactured in the United States of America
ISBN: 0-533-13593-1

Library of Congress Catalog Card No.: 00-91507

0 9 8 7 6 5 4 3 2

To my daughters,
Andrea, Carmelita, and Karen

My grandchildren, Duan, LaDonna, Julian,
Tonya, Tamara, Shavise, Eddie and Corey

The memory of my sister,
Demetris Poplar Harris

Contents

Acknowledgments

Grateful acknowledgment is given for the contributions of Murcie Poplar Lavender—Illustrator, Melvin L. Poplar, Sr.—Public relations advisor, and Mignonne Radja—Editor.

Special thanks to my husband, Henry, and Dr. Jack Kamen for encouraging me to write and publish this book.

Zero the Hero

Introduction

Have you ever heard any of these comments, or similar comments?

You are *too* SKINNY!

You are *too* FAT!

1

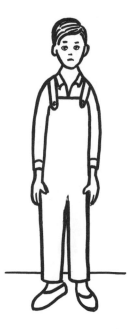

You are *too* TALL!

You are *too* SHORT!

Your hair is *too* SHORT!

Your legs are BOWED!

Your nose is *too* WIDE!

Your mouth is *too* BIG!

Your head is *too* BIG!

Your skin is BUMPY!

You STUTTER!

You read *too* SLOWLY!

How did these comments make you feel about yourself? Maybe, mean things have been said about family members and friends. How did they feel? Perhaps you have been told, as I have, that you are worthless, nothing, you would never be anything. You are just ZERO.

If you don't feel good about yourself, my autobiography is just for you. I want to tell you how I became a HERO. You see, I, ZERO, was not always a HERO. At least, I didn't believe so.

0 (zero)
1
Now that I'm looked up to   2
3
4

4
3
and looked down on   2
1
0 (zero)

and can be placed to the right of a number
like —> 5<u>0</u>
or to the left of a number like <— <u>0</u>9

I'm pretty important. No matter where someone looks, there's always a ZERO.

Listen to me tell my own story, and you, too, will realize that you *do* have worth. You, too, are a HERO.

My Story

One afternoon, nine years ago to be exact, I sat on my front steps crying.

I was dejected, debased, demeaned, defeated, discouraged, and all the other words that make one feel like zero. I knew I was one of the digits in the whole number family, but, boy! I was treated differently. No one wanted to talk to me or be my friend. I was not respected.

Every day, I would hear others say, "Oh, he's nothing; he's just a zero." I felt whole. When I looked in the mirror, I looked complete. Yet, people made me feel like a fraction—less than one. Whenever someone was told to count, he began saying 1, 2, 3. . . . I was just skipped over as if I were invisible and didn't count at all. I was included in a set of whole numbers—sort of like the subject *you* that's understood. I was taken for granted.

It pleased the children in Numberland to tease me and make me cry. The more they teased me, the more I cried. Adults, too, thought of me as an outcast. Although they wouldn't voice it, they would think to themselves as they saw me, *Oh, how skinny! I wonder if his parents feed him enough? What an enormous head! I wonder what's in it?*

One parent, Four's mom, actually made a mistake and voiced this thought in Four's presence: "My, Zero certainly does have a big

head! I wonder if anything is working in it?"
Four picked up on that unkind comment
immediately. The next time he saw me he said,
"Hey, Zero, you sure have a big head. Is
anything working in it?" What was not readily
apparent to me then was that those comments
were going around and around somewhere in
my head—even when I was not in the presence
of others.

Such was the case one snowy day in
Numberland. Many neighborhood children were
outside enjoying their sleds. I could hear their
laughter and jubilant shouts. I knew I wasn't
welcome to play with them; it was too cold to sit
on the front steps. So, I just sat indoors
watching them at play through the window.

After a time, I grew weary of watching the

other Numberland kids play. I sprawled out in a big chair nearby. Dad had gone to work, and Mom was in the kitchen cooking. I sat very quietly; that's when it happened. Suddenly, many thoughts and ideas began to fill my head. First, I heard, "Hey! Zero, you have a big head. I wonder if anything is in it?" Then, I heard, "Yes, you have a mind. Of course you have many thoughts. You can think. You can use your mind, too. People call you nobody, but you are really somebody. You *are* important. The other numbers are really jealous because you come before them. They want to tease you and make you feel inferior because they know that you are superior to them. We are all different, unique and have value."

The more I began thinking these last thoughts, the better I felt. A sense of pride arose in me, and I stopped crying. Maybe my head seems big and ugly to others, but something beautiful was happening to me. It seemed that I had more room to have more thoughts. The good, positive thoughts had begun to push out the bad, negative thoughts. *The bigger my head,* I thought, *the more thoughts and ideas I can get into it. But, I must determine what kind of thoughts and ideas should be allowed to enter.* I became so comfortable with this type of thinking that I fell asleep and began dreaming.

My Dream—Reality

I saw a Numberland helper who was an expert with computers and the Internet. He said, "Zero, type www.Z-E-R-O.com" and I did. The first thing that came on the computer screen was a place-value chart that looked like this:

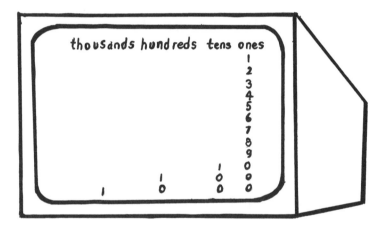

The information in the chart showed me that I was necessary to write the numeral 10 and any multiple of 10. Wow! This really made me feel important! Our number system is based on ten, and I'm needed to write the numeral 10. The computer screen showed that I had unusual powers in terms of position. I could stand to the right of a number and reproduce many of myself with commas increasing the number's value. I could reproduce myself and stand to the left of a number, decreasing or diminishing its value with the aid of a decimal point.

The screen looked like this:

10	ten
100	one hundred
1,000	one thousand
10,000	ten thousand . . .

.01	one hundredth
.001	one thousandth
.0001	one ten thousandth . . .

Next, the screen showed three scales. There was a scale like one in the produce section in a supermarket,

a scale like one in the doctor's office,

and one like we have in our bathroom.

No matter how each scale looked, it had a zero as the starting point for weighing. *Hey, I thought. I have to be recognized before things are weighed. I am important.*

I saw a ruler that showed measurements from 1 to 12 inches.

Although I didn't see a zero, I was not surprised because I'm not always recognized. I learned in school that we start measuring from the edge of the ruler to get amounts. As long as I know that zero is understood, I know that I have value.

After seeing the ruler, I saw a telephone.

I noticed that zero was the only digit that could be used by itself to dial for assistance. For other help, you had to dial at least three digits like: 911 or 411.

I saw other things on the screen that I had learned in school. For instance, I can reproduce twice to the right of 8 to get 1-800 number. This helps people to make toll-free calls.

I saw a globe and map of the world.

In the center of both was a line labeled "equator." Next to the word equator was a zero

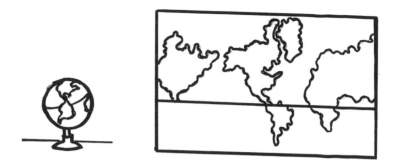

(0). Great! I'm used to divide the Northern
Hemisphere from the Southern Hemisphere.

A classroom setting appeared. Children
were practicing the capital (O) and small letter
(o) from a handwriting lesson on the board.

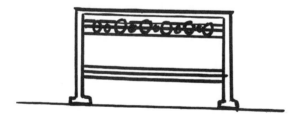

It occurred to me that I'm the only digit
that looks like a letter in the alphabet. I look
like the letter "O." Some people get us mixed up
when saying telephone numbers. Sometimes
they say "O" instead of zero.

After the handwriting lesson, I saw my

shape. It had no beginning or ending. It suggested non-stopping, continuance or infinity.

Some numbers were in columns and needed assistance. They needed someone to hold some places or substitute for them. I could hold a position in any place value.

10—I could hold the ones' place
100—I could hold both the ones' and tens' places . . .

I could be counted on because I was neither positive nor negative. I showed neutrality.

I saw that I was also used in skip-counting by 10s.

10, 20, 30, 40, 50. . . .

When one had to estimate or round numbers, I proved to be invaluable, such as when rounding to the nearest ten:

47 to 50, 42 to 40, 58 to 60. . . .

The meteorologists used my name in winter weather reports. The temperature in some places was many degrees below zero, and in others it was many degrees above zero. When someone wanted to write degrees, he made me smaller, but I was still above the number to the right: 68°. Small or large, I was still present and had value.

I saw a newspaper article advertising furniture, electronics, and appliances. What really caught my eye was my name in bold print; it gave people seven extra months before they had to pay the bill. It said "0" interest and "0" payments.

Last, I saw a % sign. Some people were buying items on sale. Some were 30% off, 50% off. . . . Without two of me, there was no way to show a percent sign.

After seeing my importance as a whole number, the Numberland helper instructed me to turn the computer off. I was now proud to be a zero.

As I awakened, I heard Mom calling me. She suggested that I get information for my math report from the computer. I went into the den where we kept the computer. Before doing my homework, I thought I'd be curious and type in www.Z-E-R-0.com on the computer, as the Numberland helper in my dream had told me. To my amazement, everything I saw in my dream was listed on the monitor. My dream wasn't really a dream, but reality. I *am* a HERO.

My Advice

Just as I realized that I AM A HERO, you can know the same thing about yourself. Whose opinion counts about you anyway? Sure, it's your opinion. If I can add up my zero points and find value, certainly you can add your pluses. Let's see, if you are skinny, fat, or your legs are bowed, you can still walk, exercise, and carry on your bodily functions as others. If your hair is short, it can be styled just to fit your unique personality. If your nose is big, you have more space to help with your breathing. If your mouth is big, you have more room for saying thank you, and compliments, and more room from which productive conversations can proceed. If your head is big, as mine is, you have so much more space to incubate ideas. If your skin is bumpy, you do have a covering to protect you from infections. OK, you stutter; you can be understood and can produce sustained sounds. You read slowly, but with practice, you can increase your speed.

Now that you've gotten a better image of yourself, you can clearly see that you DO have talent. You've had it all the time. **YOU, TOO, ARE A HERO.**

REMEMBER: "If someone ever says something negative about you, or if you ever think something negative about yourself, just think of me, ZERO, and the power I have in Numberland: I am neither positive nor negative, but wide open for you to look through and see how to cancel any negative opinions you hold about yourself. Just use the reciprocal of negative, which is positive, and that thought or opinion will be canceled. That negative will become *zero.*"

My Future

What will the new millennium bring? What about Y2K? Well, I think computers might have problems with "0" in the year 2000. The computers might think that it's the year 1900 instead of 2000. Many services that are computerized might be hampered or interrupted. Boy! People will really know my importance, then. If I'm not handled properly, I have the power to literally "shut-down" major operations.

I know now what the whole world *will then know,* that **I AM A HERO.**

About the Author

Venetia Poplar Brown

Born in Gary, Indiana. Graduated from Roosevelt High
School as valedictorian—1950;

Attended and received degrees from Indiana University,
School of Education: Bachelor of Science (B.S.) in
Education and Master of Science (M.S.) in
Education;

Taught Elementary Education for thirty three years in
the Gary Community School Corp., Gary, Indiana;

Developed curriculum for ELKA Child Educational
Center (a pre-school center with four locations
serving Northwest Indiana). Served as Elka's
Program Director for seventeen years (1968–1985);

Serves as a Board Member and Curriculum Director for
Children's Art Institute, Inc., Gary, Indiana;

Offers tutorial service and uses creativity in teaching.
Because ideas and methods can be tailor-made to
meet individual needs, tutoring is perceived as a
challenge;

Believes that each student should dictate how he/she
learns best. In terms of education, the students'
learning styles are their inalienable rights to life,
liberty, and the pursuit of happiness;

Believes that each student is endowed with talents, has
acquired skills and possesses numerous ideas that
must be shared; and

Founded ACK Educational Center in 1994; a non-profit

establishment that provided a positive environment in which a student could learn, share, and grow.

Venetia Poplar Brown resides in Gary, Indiana with her husband (Henry Brown), a financial counselor.